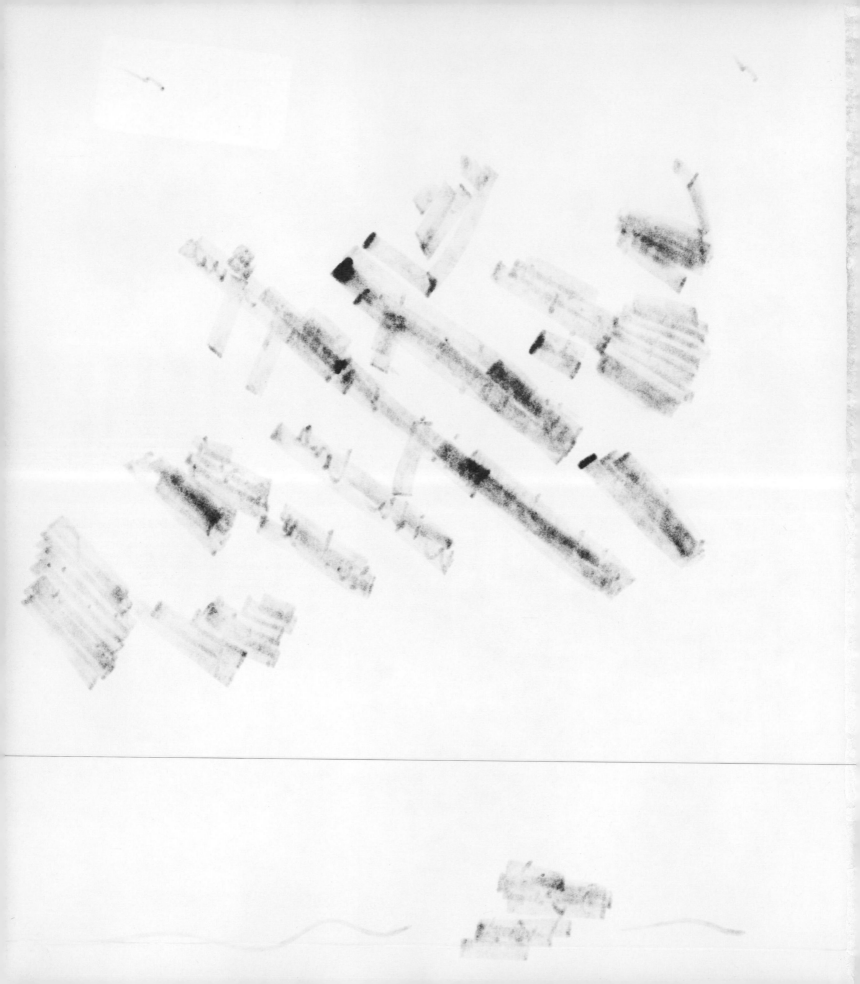

For Claude

— LYN

*For Charity, Dean,
and the real twins,
Edward and Quentin.*

— STEPHEN

WING-A-DING

by Lyn Littlefield Hoopes

Illustrated by Stephen Gammell

Little, Brown and Company
Boston Toronto London

The day Jack threw his wing-a-ding
   the very first fling
it stuck in the branches of the Willoughbys' tree.

"Wing-a-ding, you dumb thing!" said Jack.

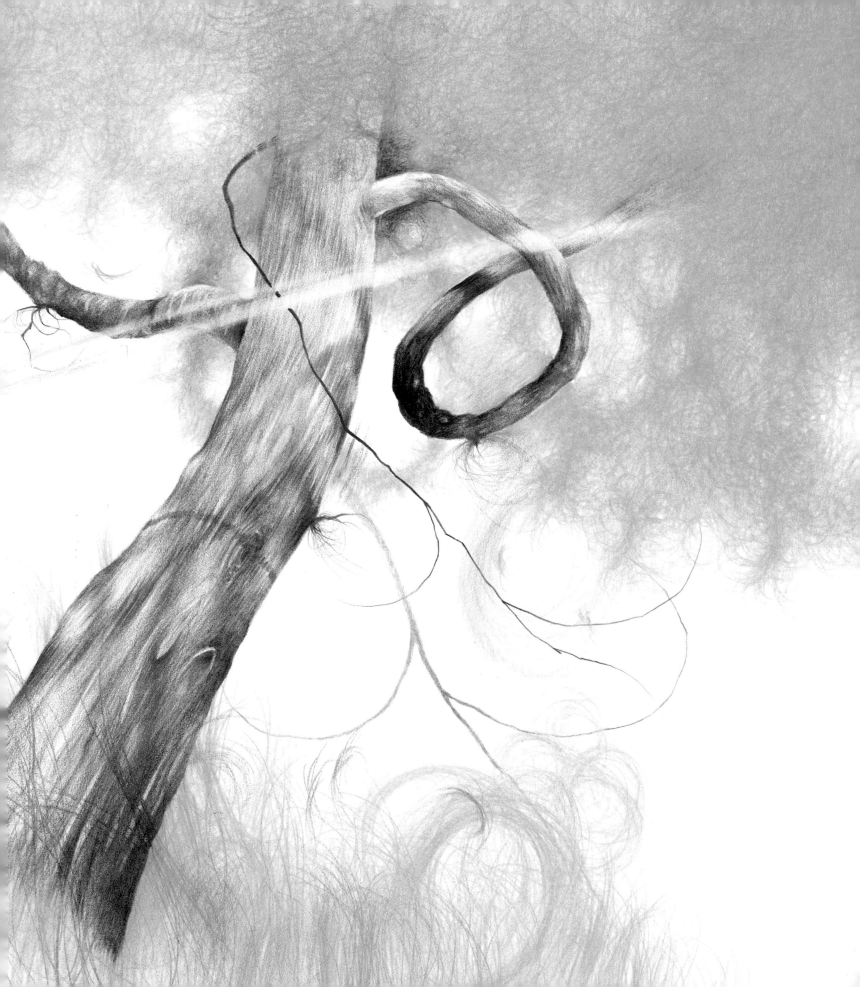

The wing-a-ding hung
high above his head;
Jack was looking for a rope
when along came Fred.

Fred grabbed ahold of the Willoughbys' tree;
he shook and he shook
but it wouldn't jump free.

"Wing-a-ding, you dumb thing!" said Jack.

Well, a ladder might do;
he could climb and hang;
but here was Miguel
with his boomerang.

He gave it a snap;
he gave it a fling.
It looped and it wrapped
round the wing-a-ding.

"Wing-a-ding, you dumb thing!" said Jack.

Yes, a ladder could do,
he might get it like that;
but here was Sue
with her scrawny cat.

"Fetch, Skinny," yelled Sue.
Skinny shinnied up a branch and cried
"Mewww!"

Now what would do
for a wing-a-ding,
a boomerang,
and a cat crying
"Mewww"?

Samantha came along with her fishing pole.
"Look at me," she said,
as she cast her line

Snap
Twang

there was the bobber
on the boomerang!

Now what would do
for a wing-a-ding,
a boomerang,
a bobber,
and a cat crying
"Mewww"?

Mrs. Penny ran over with her big porch broom.
Jack climbed on Fred.
"Get it, Skinny," Sue said.

Cam came up with her mini-tramp,
bounced, and caught the nearest branch.
She hung by her knees like a chimpanzee.
She swung and swung but it wouldn't come free.

The twins whizzed by
on their tandem bike.
"We'll be back," said Mac.
"Wait," said Mike.

They circled round in their cowboy suits.
Mac threw a lasso.
Mike tossed his boots. . .

Now here was a boot,
a bobber,
and a boomerang
hanging from the ring of a wing-a-ding,
the lasso around Jack,
up on Fred's back,
and Cam, like a chimpanzee,
swinging from the branches of the Willoughbys' tree.

"Wing-a-ding, you dumb thing," said Jack.

Scooter skidded in
with his laser guns.

"Shoot it!" he shouted.
   "I'm hot!"

He aimed and shot.

"Snag it!" yelled Sam.
"Shake it!" said Fred.
"Squirt it!" yelled Mac.
Jack ducked his head.

Mike grabbed the hose,
Mac opened the spray,
the cat cried *"Mewww!"*
and leapt away.

"Wing-a-ding, you ding-a-ling!" shouted Jack.

What would do?
What would it take?

"What we need," said Sue,
"is a superlong rake."

"A crane," yelled Mike,
"a skyhook, a plane."

"A helicopter," said Fred.
"Or a hurricane."

"A giraffe," said Cam. "A tyrannosaurus!"

Maralee skated in
to watch the chorus.

She spun round twice,
round in a ring,
then quietly
she began to sing.

*"Wing-a-ding, high and free,
way up in the Willoughbys' tree,
won't you please fly down to me?"*

Fred started singing, and Miguel and Sue,
Mrs. Penny piped in; the twins did too.
They made a ring round the Willoughbys' tree,
and they all sang with Maralee.

"Wing-a-ding, fly down to me!"

The postman stopped
when he heard their song;
the diaper man, he hummed along.
Now Scooter dropped his gun,
and they all sang, every one.

"Wing-a-ding, fly down to me. . . ."

"Now come along, wing-a-ding," called Mrs. Penny.

"Wing-a-ding, you're a *good* thing," whispered Jack.

And,

was it the wind that blew?
No one knew,

but suddenly . . .

the **wing-a-ding**

FLEW!

First Edition

Library of Congress Cataloging-in-Publication Data

Hoopes, Lyn Littlefield.
  Wing-a-ding / by Lyn Littlefield Hoopes; illustrated by
Stephen Gammell.
      p.   cm.
  Summary: Jack's efforts to free his toy wing-a-ding from
the branches of a tree soon involve the increasingly outra-
geous efforts of friends, neighbors, and passersby.
  ISBN 0-316-37237-4
  [1. Toys — Fiction. 2. Stories in rhyme.] I. Gammell,
Stephen, ill. II. Title.
PZ8.3.H77Wi   1990   89-38467
[E] — dc20   CIP
                                            AC

Joy Street Books are published
by Little, Brown and Company (Inc.)

10 9 8 7 6 5 4 3 2 1

WOR

Published simultaneously in Canada
by Little, Brown & Company (Canada) Limited

Printed in the United States of America